THE HUNT FOR CORONA

THE HUNT for CORONA

FAHAD ALFALASI

FLASH STORIES

Published by: Gulf Book Service Ltd
            20-22 Wenlock Road, London.
            NI 7GU
            UK
            Email: info@gulfbooks.co.uk

ISBN: 978-1-7397687-8-2 (Print)
978-1-7397687-9-9 (E-book)
Year: 2022

Social Media Username: AUfahadalfalasi
www.fahadalfalasi.com

Dedication

*To all victims of COVID-19,
a virus that, alas, has achieved something
many states have not:
it has spread equality without regard to
gender, color, or status.*

CONTENTS

PROLOGUE

He was in the midst of a dream that bore no resemblance to any other. Some say dreams are revelations are granted to us by divine power, yet others disagree, claiming that they are nothing but intimidations by Satan; while scientists insist they are simply a reflection of our daily lives. For him, it was not any of those probabilities but a series of unpleasant confrontations.

First, he had seen his sister Artemis tie him up.

"How could you?! I'm your brother!"

As she began tying his feet, she replied, "I am not only your sister, but also your twin. Yet we're juxtaposed, like fire and rain... you live carnally, I live chastely. I'm doing what is best for us!" And before long, she vanished.

Afterwards, and before Apollo could figure out was going on, a girl started to materialize.

"Cassandra! My love!"

"Not anymore!" she retorted while covering his mouth with a strip. "After I resisted you, you cursed me with the most shameful mark a woman could have; a lack of credibility. And thus I became the woman who cries when those I cherish doubt my prophecies, then sheds tears of blood when they face their doom. Because of you, I am powerless to prevent their demise, but understand this: if nobody will believe what comes out of my mouth, nobody will hear what comes out of your mouth from now on!" She double-checked the strip before she disappeared.

Finally, another girl came into sight. Apollo started shaking and mumbling in astonishment.

"Relax! Yes, I'm Daphne, I too am a lover, but only of life—of nature, of all that is green, of all that is blue. I climb mountains and swim rivers, but I lost it all because of you. And before you cursed me, I foolishly cursed myself, by transforming into a tree, a piece of nature that I always adored, and by doing so I lost myself. But now I'm regaining my freedom and myself, and you can kiss my love goodbye!" And before long, she melted away.

Apollo awoke, shuddering. His heart pounded and his forehead was sweaty. It had been one hell of a nightmare. Some dreams were worse than a near-death experience. He hurried to reassure himself by touching his head, shortly after, he realized that the dream was no dream at all. A crown of bay leaves that he wore day and night transformed to foliage.

He ran toward the bay laurel tree but could find the only remains of its trunk and roots. His eyes quickly darted toward the river that once was. Its water was now dried up, its fish flittering on the muddy bottom. It made him certain that Daphne had run away.

He remembered when he had fallen madly in love with her. Since she had sworn to remain a virgin, she refused to accept his advances. So, he decided to hunt her, but right at the moment he caught her, she turned into a laurel tree.

He was determined to go after her. Attempting to locate her right away, he fired a volley of arrows at her, tipped with an infinitesimal yet detrimental curse.

And thus, Corona spread wherever she fled.

She knew she had to roam over all the Earth so that finding her would be unachievable.

The hunt for Daphne began.

1.

OLD BUDDIES CLUB

On Earth, a torrent of raindrops fell from amorphous clouds and pounded the avenue. These were not the kind of gray-swaying-to-black clouds that you see when a storm is about to hit. This was an ink black sky roaring with thunder, unloading its weight onto the ground like gunshots. You could almost see fractions of your face reflecting in the winding puddles scattered across the brick-paved walkway. Suddenly, two flaming sparks burst in the middle of one puddle, oddly unextinguished—the sparks emanated from the red heels of a ravishing lass heading through the crowd towards a buzzing club—a referral from her friend Cassandra—at the far end of the avenue.

She took a deep breath to settle her excitement as she pushed open the club's door. She was eager to hear about the experiences of her peers. Even a loser might unknowingly give a word of advice, she supposed.

She walked into the club nonchalantly, with a toss of golden braids woven into her hair, which fell below her padded shoulders. Her eyes brightened and her face gleamed with a glowing smile when she noticed how crowded the place was.

"This will surely make my mission a lot easier," she thought to herself.

She sat herself at a round glass table where two men were seated, facing each other uneasily. One was a tall man, skinny as a sugarcane. The other was short and round, plump as a watermelon. They greeted her eagerly, with giddiness caused by her casual confidence and charm.

"Have you been waiting for me for long?" Without waiting for an answer, she continued, "You've apparently made good use of your time." She looked at two glasses, one filled with a shimmering golden drink and the other with a ruby-red one. "Odd how your tastes part ways when one cause unites you." She played idly with her braids.

Trying to draw her attention to himself, the skinny man said, "My pal here says he's more successful than me. Can you believe that?"

"Because it's true," the chubby man said, giving a proud nod.

The skinny man cuffed his companion on the head.

The woman tossed her hair. "Enough, you two! I haven't come all the way here to listen to this nonsense. I need a game plan."

The chubby man sipped his ruby-red drink. "It's simple. Keep a low profile, and strike fast and hard before anyone notices you."

The other man sighed. "Here's some good advice: do what you have to do, but quietly and efficiently."

"How so? Mister...?" She paused as clouds of smoke rose up from her vape. "What may I call you?"

The skinny man rushed to answer first. "SARS, it is. And I managed in months what took that fella years to accomplish."

"Fella? I beg your pardon! I have a name and it's Ebola."

"Even my name is more substantial than yours," SARS said, disdain clear in his voice. "Ebola," he mumbled under his breath, laughing to himself.

The woman stood up. "You two are so predictable. Thanks for the advice. I have to go now."

"You haven't told us your name!" Both men leaned forward intently.

"Corona," she said, formally shaking their hands.

She started to walk away, then looked back, clubgoers passing closely by her. "I'll give you two some genuine advice in exchange." Her words were as cold as dry ice. "Accomplish your mission while your prey is naively smiling at you."

Then she headed through the crowd back toward the door, leaving Ebola and SARS clueless as to what she was hinting at.

Before they could carry on drinking, a severe thunderclap overtook their senses. Not long after this, fever dominated their bodies, accompanied by a series of dry coughs that left them dangerously short of breath. Panicking now, their eyes screamed for help, begging anyone to come to their rescue. They realized later that Corona is not a typical kind of virus.

Nobody did. People stood back—in horror. And who would dare to step closer? Who was endowed with so great a courage? Who wished to lose their lives to the crown bearer? To Corona?

2.

A BATTLE ON
TWO FRONTS

Dust it may be, except that no cosmic dust flares. It may be a star, but stars don't twinkle left and right. Thus, it is beyond a shadow of a doubt a comet. Then again, since when do comets carry people? A spacecraft it must be then. It is one indeed. But it would be an understatement to refer to such a vast presence as a mere vehicle. Closer in size to a meteor and resembling a star in its glowing radiance, it tore by like a flash on its way to infiltrate the atmosphere of planet Earth— the planet of the disobedient, as labeled by the passengers on this majestic spacecraft.

Inside, Vittorio, the stately commander with his tall stature and slender frame, was surrounded by large screens showing the data to a dozen watching soldiers and officers. With a scepter that he'd taken as his own after overtaking Mars, slaying its king and scattering its people, he pointed toward Earth on one of the screens.

"Finally, no obstacle is left ahead of us. We can now rule every human on this arrogant planet," he said in a hissing voice.

"Those snobs failed to even set foot on any planet other than the moon!" an officer added.

Vittorio sneered. "These selfish creatures have been fighting each other for thousands of years. They could never win. Those who fail to triumph over their desires could never triumph over their enemies."

"Sir, I'm afraid I bear news of... puzzling changes," said a pilot, already perspiring.

"What do you mean?" Displeasure was clear in Vittorio's voice.

"Armies all over planet Earth are in a state of alert," the pilot continued. "Armed police are roaming the streets and citizens are locked down in their homes."

"Could it be that the humans have detected our arrival?" Vittorio tapped angrily on the screen.

"They don't stand a chance against us," said the pilot with conviction. "Their defeat is certain."

"Be silent! You will never understand humans better than I do. They are far more cunning and vile than you think. Retreat to our bases! I will not risk my forces."

Just as suddenly as it had appeared, the spacecraft disappeared again into outer space, as if a black hole had swallowed it. Thus, danger ceased to be—for a while.

Meanwhile, in an apartment on planet Earth, another conflict was on the verge of breaking out. There was Tom, head down, eyes focused on his iPad, watching a movie. Carrying a laptop, his father—who was in the middle of an online meeting with his head office in Japan—stormed into the living room. He wore a business jacket on top and sweatpants on the bottom. "It's time you went to sleep!" he said impatiently.

"Just another fifteen minutes!" Tom begged.

"What difference would a quarter of an hour make?"

"A lot! That's the time left till the end of the movie."

"Is it educational?" his father asked.

"Of course!" Tom voiced passionately. "It's about aliens invading the Earth."

His father sighed. "Are you wasting your time watching more of this fictitious stuff?" He all but dragged Tom, whose eyes were still locked onto his iPad, into his bedroom. "I wish aliens *would* invade us. Maybe they would fix us a cure for this pandemic, so I no longer have to teach you myself at home."

3.

WINGLESS PLANE

An overcrowded queue of people grumbled before a business lounge buffet at Heathrow Airport. Standing at the very front of the line was Ali. His eyes couldn't help but wander left and right across the various breakfast dishes on display, most of them unhealthy delicacies and a few healthy but certainly not tasty ones. A British man standing behind him cleared his throat, breaking Ali out of his musings.

"Ahem! Excuse me, I suggest you go for the continental. It's rich in flavor but light on the stomach," said the British man as Ali turned to face him.

At that moment, Ali felt the urge to make a quick decision. He would skip breakfast for a single loaf of bread, although this only puzzled him all the more as he lost himself in a veritable ocean of bread of all varieties and sizes. Suddenly, he heard another cough from behind him.

"Brown bread! High in nutrients and fiber!"

An endless stream of impatient coughs ensued from everyone waiting their turn, so Ali was forced to take whatever his hands landed on before hurrying to leave. Finally, the line moved ahead like a row of falling dominoes.

In a lounge flooded with travelers from all corners of the world because of the recent outbreak of COVID-19, Ali was finally able to find himself a table. Shortly after, the British man who had stood behind him in line arrived, asking if they could share. They chatted as they ate—after all, food naturally tastes better when enjoyed with company.

Ali initiated the conversation. "I came to London for a medical exam, and it was found that I had to undergo surgery. However, I couldn't go through with it. I have to return to Dubai to complete a business deal."

Empathizing with him, the British man said, "What good will a business deal do when you don't have the strength to operate it?"

"My partner bore my travel expenses from Dubai; I can't let him down. My absence would leave a bad impression," Ali explained.

The British man seemed unconvinced. It was now his turn to tell his story. "My mother's birthday coincided with my vacation, so I asked my eldest brother, who currently resides in Dubai, to postpone my return. But he refused, as he'd already set up a date with his business partner in their coffeehouse business."

Sounding indignant, Ali said, "For such an exceptional occasion, he should be more understanding."

"The thing is, I'm in charge of our coffee shop opening."

Suddenly, a voice came from the loudspeakers, interrupting their conversation. "To all travelers, we are very sorry to announce that all remaining flights are canceled due to the spread of COVID-19."

Confusion spread and escalated among the travelers, who soon split into two teams. One rushed to call family members and loved ones, while the other sought help from the information center.

"This is my chance!" said the British man. "I'll contact my brother about the situation. He'll have to meet his partner without me."

Ali agreed. "And I'll let my partner know that I won't be returning soon, since I'll be able to have that surgery now. Health always comes first, as you said."

No definitive information was coming from the information desk. Nobody seemed to know when flights would resume. The British man made the call to his brother to update him. "Hi, Topher! It seems I've gotten stuck at the airport, but as luck would have it, I get the chance to celebrate Mom's birthday!"

A few seconds later, Ali's mobile rang. "Hello, Christopher!" he answered. "Yes, what you heard is true, we're grounded." He soon hung up, his brows furrowed.

"What's with the question mark on your face?" asked the British man, who looked at him with barely suppressed amusement.

"How did my partner get the news so fast?" He shook his head in amazement.

"Bad news travels fast, especially when it's received by one's brother!" the British man replied with a beam of pleasure.

Ali ran out of patience. "What brother? My partner's name is Christopher, and I heard you talking to your brother. His name... something that started with *T*, wasn't it?" He scratched his head in bewilderment.

"Topher! Don't you know it's a nickname for Christopher?" said the British man, still grinning cheerfully.

"Wait, so that means *you're* Clark?"

They shook hands warmly, and Clark invited Ali to stay at his place until their wingless plane grew wings again.

Thus it was that Clark's mother had two people celebrating her birthday instead of one—while taking all necessary precautions, of course.

4.

NIGHTFALL VISITOR

The buzzing of the busy telephone line almost deafened Jacob's ears. His rigid figure could barely contain the anxious fluttering in his chest. As a policeman, he naturally amplified potential risks, especially when it came to the person he loved most, his wife. And with this abnormal situation of COVID-19, it was absolutely normal for his palpitating heart to overshadow the buzzing of the phone, no matter how loud. His heart skipped a beat every time he messaged her but received no response. "Now I know how the wound of the soul cuts deeper than that of the body," he thought. His fear for her grew slowly until it completely wore him down, baring its fangs.

Standing alone, he threw his mobile as though aiming at his fears, yelling to himself as loudly as he possibly could: "Where are you, Emma?"

At the same time, back at home, Emma whispered into the phone as if someone was eavesdropping on her. "No!

This has to be dealt with before dawn. My husband can't know about this."

"Lieutenant, this is negligence! How could you forget to bring your pager? Especially at curfew time?"

"My apologies, sir!" Jacob answered. "I forgot it because—"

"We don't have time for your excuses now. Bring it back here, and never repeat the same mistake again!"

"Yes, sir!"

Jacob used the pager excuse to race back home, inhaling anxiety and exhaling resentment.

At home, the doorbell rang. Emma rushed to answer it.

A few moments later, she went outside to look for something, but the wind pushed the door shut. Her mobile was left inside, and she couldn't figure out a way back in. Trapped in the biting cold, Emma looked around wildly, hoping not to have to be outside for too long so as not to draw any attention to herself. But suddenly someone grabbed her by the arm.

"You're hurting me!" she screamed.

It was obvious that Jacob's fear had turned to anger. "You hurt me, too! Why didn't you reply to any of my messages or calls?" he yelled. Emma stumbled in the face of Jacob's anger. "And what are you doing outside at this hour? It's curfew time!"

"Let me explain!"

Before she could begin to rationalize her defense, Jacob noticed a man on his bedroom balcony. He had a medical mask, and it seemed as though he was desperately seeking an exit.

Pointing his gun at him, Jacob exploded, "This situation needs no explanation!" Now his tone shifted from anger to fury.

Terrified, the masked man on the balcony rushed back inside.

Jacob ran toward the house, Emma following. When presented with a locked door, Jacob didn't hesitate to kick it down. As soon as he broke into the room, the masked man fell to his knees, raising his trembling hands in surrender.

"Don't shoot! He's unarmed!" Emma yelled.

"Are you sympathizing with him now?" Jacob answered derisively. He ordered the man to show his face, and as the mask was slowly removed, it revealed a figure noticeably over seventy years old.

Jacob turned to Emma, baffled. "Who are you?" he asked, returning his attention to the stranger. "And what are you doing in my house?"

Flustered and aghast at what had happened, the old man was unable to utter a single word. As Emma helped him up, she felt him shaking all over and helped him to settle on the edge of the bed.

"I'm homeless. I once had a son . . ." He paused for a moment. "But he abandoned me long ago. During the curfew, I have been sneaking into houses seeking shelter. Eventually, fate led me here... to your home."

Filled with remorse, Jacob looked at Emma. "What were you doing outside though?"

Emma glanced at an elegant gift box placed neatly on the bed, flowers strewn around it.

"A cake?" Jacob exclaimed as he opened the box.

"It's your birthday cake. The carrier couldn't deliver it sooner because of the checkpoints set up to monitor the curfew. But I noticed the birthday card I ordered was missing, so I put the cake box on the bed and went to look for it outside. That's when you startled me, and then..."

Stooping down, Jacob kissed her hand, then stood back up to kiss her forehead, begging for forgiveness. "I'm so sorry. The busy phone line filled my mind with doubts, and seeing you outside like that worried me even more. Then the presence of this man blinded me completely."

"That's not an excuse!"

"It isn't," he admitted, while opening the box. "But it seems the delivery man deceived you. That's half a cake in the box!"

"Er, that's my fault," the old man interrupted. "I was hungry, and when I saw your wife in the yard busy looking for something while the door was wide open, I took the chance and ran inside to have my shelter for the night. I was lucky enough to enter before the wind slammed the door shut. I hope you have it in you to forgive me, just as your loyal wife forgave you."

"Well, you're forgiven if you accept his apology," Emma spoke to Jacob as she wiped away her tears.

Embracing his wife, Jacob said, "Of course, and I'll even forgive myself if you accept my apology, Emma. You too, sir. I invite you to celebrate with us. And I promise to help you look for a place that meets your needs tomorrow."

Although the curfew had brought about much distress to some, it without question helped others, the first of whom was this homeless old man. Ultimately, good and bad are just opposite sides of the same coin.

5.

BUY & SQUANDER STORE

In a downtown supermarket, the headstrong Sophia and her husband greeted their neighbors, the quick-tempered Ava and her husband. "We didn't expect to see you here so early in the morning!"

"Neither did we!" Ava replied swiftly.

"So, what brings you here?" asked her husband, despite the obvious answer.

"Food! What else could it be?" Sophia and her husband answered simultaneously.

After exchanging brief compliments, the two couples walked through the produce section, where most shelves stood empty. Then each couple took a different aisle, although much to their amazement, they bumped into each other once again in the health and hygiene section.

"Didn't you say you were going to the produce section?" Ava exclaimed.

"Indeed, we were," Sophia responded confidently. "It was overcrowded though, so we had to change direction through this aisle. What about you?"

Ava's husband stuttered, so Ava had to improvise. With a fake smile, she said, "That's exactly what happened with us!" The couples then parted for a second time.

As Sophia was examining the shelves, they bumped into Ava yet again, who, along with her husband, looked exhausted from stacking their carts with hand sanitizer.

"It isn't fair to clear out these shelves into your basket!" Sophia protested.

Suddenly, they were scrapping over packs of sanitizer that landed on the ground around them, causing a great disturbance and even greater embarrassment. The husbands had no choice but to intervene.

The first one pleaded, "Break it off, you two! You're embarrassing us!"

"Please calm down! We can split them in half," the second one added.

The couples agreed to share what was left, knowing they couldn't afford to lose what had become as precious as gold. As Ava's husband checked the price on one of the packs, he pondered aloud, "That's only fifty smackers! We'll be rolling in it with this price."

Sophia's husband gasped, "Ours has a price tag of a hundred dollars!"

Both now realized there were two different brands with different prices. The tension was thick, and for the second time, the husbands had to intervene to evenly split the cheapest packs and the most expensive ones.

A few minutes later, Ava and her husband made it to the front of the checkout line.

"That's a good pile of hand sanitizers!" Ava commented as the cashier scanned their items.

"That comes to a thousand dollars," the cashier concluded.

Ava was taken aback. "Wait, how come? We didn't take enough to cost that much!"

The cashier lady explained, pointing at the packs, "You're buying two brands. This one costs one hundred dollars and that one costs two hundred."

"You must be mistaken!" Ava's husband sputtered. "The labels say only fifty dollars for this kind and a hundred for that one."

"We may have forgotten to change labels. The supplier of the fifty-dollar brand increased their price after it became scarce in the market, so its price jumped to two hundred dollars, whereas the hundred-dollar brand remained the same."

Ava and her husband rushed to put the "fifty-dollar" packs back on the shelves. Still in the aisle, Sophia was flabbergasted. "Why are you returning them?"

Ava made an effort to sound apologetic. "Those in need are more deserving."

"All shoppers should look up to you," Sophia said, trying to sound convincing.

As soon as Ava and her husband left, the other couple hurried to replace the hundred-dollar packs they'd taken with those that they thought cost fifty dollars.

A few minutes later, the two couples met once again in the supermarket parking lot, where Ava and her husband were celebrating their successful deal. Sophia was annoyed at first, telling them that the price of the once-cheaper packs had been changed, but that she and her husband had to buy them anyway because they were too timid to return them in front of the other shoppers.

Ava and her husband tried to show some sympathy. "It's alright. Look on the bright side—others couldn't even get their hands on a single bottle of sanitizer!"

Now Sophia seemed more convinced, commenting as she checked her bags, "At least we won't need any more of these for a while." Then she caught sight of the expiration date. "February of last year!"

Ava hurried to check the expiration date on the ones she'd purchased. "February, the year before last!" she shouted miserably.

She and her husband ran back, but the workers were already closing the supermarket doors. "All sales are final," they said, smirking. "No returns, refunds, or exchanges!"

6.

SACRED MISSION

"Infected! Could you check the result again, please? I'm sure something is wrong."

"I checked it three times. I'm sorry to inform you, but you must stay home during the quarantine period. Our medical facilities cannot handle any more patients. Goodbye."

Noah's phone slipped from his trembling hands. He fell on his knees, sweating bullets, his heart pounding like a jackhammer. He was now one of the many infected people he'd heard about in the news. It had never occurred to him, even for a second, that this news could become his reality.

His fear gradually turned into frustration, then anger. "Of all the people on the face of this planet, why did it have to infect me? Where's the justice in all this?" Then he had another thought. "But couldn't the universe have picked me for a special reason?" He found solace in that notion.

As if on a sacred mission, Noah wasted no time and spared no effort to spread the virus in every way imaginable. He clawed the ground inch by inch, pressing every elevator button, touching every metro handle, and using every handrail—everything a human hand might touch, intentionally or not.

Sometime later in an elevator, while Noah was executing justice by pressing each button with his contaminated fingers, a maskless man entered. Just as the elevator was about to go up, the unmasked man let out a cough that all but shook the ground beneath them.

"Hey, you! Can't you watch out? Don't you know we're in the middle of a deadly pandemic?" Noah shouted, aiming to cover his actions.

"I'm so sorry," the man said apologetically. "I couldn't buy a mask because of the shortage."

"Here you go!" Noah handed him a mask as if he'd done the man a favor.

"Thank you!" the man exclaimed. "But how come you're not wearing one?"

Confidently, Noah answered, "I'm simply not prone to disease." He followed this up with a cough straight toward the man's face, who didn't seem to care.

This was confusing to Noah. "What? Don't you fear Corona?"

The man smiled, watching Noah for his reaction as he stated, "Those who are infected have no reason to fear it."

Noah chuckled. "If what you're saying is true, we're alike."

He proceeded to tell his story to the man. It was a twist of fate that they shared the same story. The man told Noah how much it annoyed him that he, of all people, got infected, and that now he felt only hatred for people around him, especially those who were healthy. Together, they made up their minds to work hand in hand to spread justice the way they saw fit.

The next day, the two newfound friends were engrossed in their task by the roadside. This time, they were using each drinking fountain they came across when Noah's cell phone rang. A woman's voice spoke that sounded familiar to him. "Am I speaking to Mr. Noah?"

"I'm busy volunteering. Call me later," Noah answered, sheer indifference in his voice.

As if he hadn't said anything, the woman continued, "We're sorry to interrupt, but we're calling to inform you that an error occurred while examining your sample. It turns out that the result was negative. We're sorry again for the inconvenience—and congratulations!"

For the second time, Noah had trembling hands, was sweating bullets, and his heart pounded like a jackhammer. This time around, it was utter fear, with no place for frustration or a grudge.

His companion immediately noticed Noah's sudden change in expression. "What's wrong with you?" he said, continuing to contaminate the drinking fountain. "We don't have time for this, we're on a sacred mission!"

7.

THE FLUTIST

A famous singer, Matthew received an unceasing barrage of applause for his spectacular performance. He waved and bowed to the audience before walking off stage for a break.

The drummer rubbed his tingling hands after an over-long performance and turned to his fellow flute player. "We play our hearts out every single night, yet *he's* the one who reaps all the money at the end of the day. We barely make any ourselves. And don't even get me started on fame—we get totally brushed aside."

The flutist patted him on the shoulder. "Take it easy! You'd probably do the same thing if you were in his shoes, wouldn't you?"

Toward the end of the concert, Matthew received a phone call that upset him. He beckoned to one of his assistants, who rushed to the producer to inform him that they had to cancel the next day's concert. The news spread like wildfire through the small ensemble, leaving them in a state of shock and frustration. The guitarist wondered aloud why it would be canceled so suddenly.

"Corona!" the maestro simply replied.

"But what about our pay?" the pianist shouted.

All of them flew into a fit of rage until Matthew announced that he would pay for half of their wages from his own pocket until the pandemic came to an end.

"Is this what we get for all our hard work? I should've graduated from college like my dad advised," the pianist commented sarcastically.

The other members were quick to thank Matthew in an attempt to cover up the pianist's ungrateful comment.

During those bleak, difficult days, some peoples' stars rose, while others ended up as has-beens. Photos of medics and nurses filled every social media platform and news outlet, while singers and football players sank into oblivion. It seemed as though the cancellation of the band's musical tour due to Corona wasn't enough—the disease also broke apart the glue that kept the band intact: Matthew.

The band members all decided to visit Matthew in the hospital, except for the pianist, who was unhappy with the pay cut. They feared Matthew's reaction to this and urged the flutist to convince the pianist to go along with them, afraid that Matthew might otherwise regard his absence as a betrayal and cut off the funds promised to them. The hospital was overwhelmed with patients, and neither the singer's fame nor prestige had spared him a single bed.

When the flutist appeared, the maestro asked him nervously, "Where's the pianist?"

"I went to his house, but he wasn't there."

The maestro sighed in irritation. "Matthew will be upset that we're not all here."

With clarity and conviction, the flutist replied, "No, he won't. On the contrary, he'll be quite satisfied." He walked toward a doctor who was busy treating a patient. The minute the doctor spotted him, he welcomed the flutist with open arms.

"Do you know this doctor?" The maestro was completely baffled.

"Of course he does," the doctor answered for him. "How could the best nurse we have on staff not know me? Now, why don't we find your friend Matthew a bed?"

The other band members' jaws dropped as they realized their friend was actually a nurse who cared for patients by day and a musician who played the flute by night, allowing him to make more money.

Just as there are heroes in movies, there are heroes in reality, some of whom we see every day, and only a few shine in crisis.

8.

THE LANGUAGE OF EYES

In a clothing store, Henry was gently rubbing an off-white shirt made of linen that had caught his attention when suddenly the store door opened. This time though, Henry didn't feel the cool breeze that snuck in when customers entered and went past him, but rather a stinging chill that sunk down to his very bones. A shiver traveled up and down his body as if it was trying to fight off an infection. He turned his head and looked behind him—and that was when he saw her.

Although they'd known each other only for a short time and their relationship was limited to phone calls and messages due to Corona, he found in her everything he wanted and more, and she was glad to have a companion who appreciated her value. The pandemic didn't stop Henry from proposing to the girl of his dreams.

At her father's home, he had to wear a mask as he sat with him. After the father had finished listening to Henry, he asked his wife who sat close to him to go get their daughter.

But to Henry's surprise, three girls wearing face masks entered the room.

With a frown on his face, the father asked, "For which of these girls are you asking her hand?"

Henry could not answer—the only thing he could do was look into their eyes, realizing that he wasn't the only one whose love mattered. Their father surpassed him significantly in his love for his triplets. As much as Henry was angry at such a trick, he understood why the father had come up with such a bizarre idea to safeguard his daughters.

The father began to speak, knitting his brows. "These girls are everything in my life—in fact, they *are* my life. And I want to be assured about their future. So, if the girl you fell for is one of these three, your soul will naturally be drawn to hers, your heart to her heart, and your eyes will find hers. This is my only condition." Before Henry could comment, the father continued, "You should know that you only have one chance to make your choice. If your first choice appears to be a mistake, I will not risk handing my daughter over to someone who might repeat his mistakes. Needless to say, mistakes in love and war are beyond repair."

Henry took a deep breath as he prepared himself to pass the most crucial test of his life. His glance swept between each young lady, but that only perplexed him further.

The first girl gave him a sarcastic look, as though she was making fun of the situation... or could it be that she was his beloved, mocking his indecision? The second girl had woebegone eyes. Perhaps she felt sorry for him... or maybe *she* was his beloved and couldn't help but sympathize with him? The third girl glared with menacing eyes. For all Henry knew, it might have meant that she was irritated by the situation... or maybe it was his beloved—mad that he didn't recognize her at first sight.

Everyone's eyes were pointed toward Henry like loaded guns. All but drowning in his bewilderment, he closed his own eyes in trepidation—and this was when his subconsciousness awoke, and his soul lit up.

"I'll make up my mind once they've left the room," Henry finally said, eyes still closed.

The father regarded Henry's response as evidence of his failure and asked his daughters to leave the room. As the second girl reached the doorway, Henry sensed the exact stinging chill that had sunk down to his very bones when she entered the shop that first day they met. He shouted, "Wait!"

And indeed, she was the girl of his dreams.

"But how did you know she was the one?" the father wondered.

"When it comes to true love, the heart sees what's invisible to the eyes."

9.

A JOURNEY FOR INDULGENCE

When you caught sight of this house, the first thing you noticed was that it bore a strong resemblance to houses nearby, yet there was something about it that captivated peoples' attention. However, dust was piled up on the windowsills. Was it abandoned? Old stacks of newspapers were tossed on the porch of the doorstep. Was that an ominous sign?

Visitors to this house used to stop by daily. Then the stream of people slowly lessened to weekly, then monthly, and finally came to an end. Ultimately, people settled for phoning those in the house, but before long, even this happened less and less until the calls also came to a halt.

Three lodgers, whom decades of tribulation had humbled, decided to band together with the yearning to seek sanctuary. They soon became devoted friends in exile in the house, which they titled with a dilapidated sign: "Nursing Home."

The first man was paralyzed. He had been abandoned by his only spoiled son and his wife, the latter of whom was said to have made the former choose between her and his father. On the spur of the moment, the young man had chosen his present over his past.

The second man was mute. He had been dumped by his good-looking wife after he had given away most of his fortune to her—a common blunder made by men when it came to her. She responded logically, ditching him for a suave-looking gentleman, enjoying days filled with wine and roses.

The third man was blind and likewise abandoned by his wife, who married another after he lost his vision. She sought someone who could take care of her and not the other way around.

The age of miracles was long gone, and for that reason, the well-being of the three elderly men was expected to worsen. However, a miracle actually materialized. The bond that connected these three friends in times of peace—pre-COVID—grew even stronger in times of chaos. The blind and the mute men helped push the wheelchair for their paralyzed friend. The paralyzed and blind men worked together to cook for their mute friend, who in turn guided his blind friend wherever he desired.

Corona, being itself, visited the city without prior notice, breaking into houses unannounced. When the nurse got the news, she packed her bags, ready to go. In a tone full of self-reproach, she apologized to the three old men, explaining that she needed to travel urgently.

"I fear Corona will finish up its mission before I return," she muttered under her breath as she stepped outside.

One day, a noise that was eerily familiar to the men's ears sounded. After a considerable amount of time, they realized it was a knocking on their door.

It appeared that another miracle had come to pass. At the door were the most unexpected visitors.

At his wife's behest, the son of the paralyzed man rushed to the nursing home, seeking his father's rescue after losing his job. "Father! You never gave up on me as a child, don't give up on me now!" his brash son begged.

Deceived by her lover who stole everything she had, the mute man's wife came by as well. "Your experience in life will help you to forgive those who are inexperienced," the cheating wife said, pleading for her husband's sympathy.

The blind man's wife too whisked by; she had been cheated on by her husband with perfect vision. "I left the man who was blind in the eyes for someone who was blind in the mind. Don't make me lose them both!" the treacherous wife beseeched.

The elderly friends exchanged looks, including the blind man. Simultaneously, they responded: "Agreed!" The mute man replied with a nod. Their visitors felt on top of the world.

The mute man disappeared for a moment, bringing back two checkbooks.

The paralyzed man handed a check to his son and wife. "You can have this money under one condition: don't ever show your face here again."

Handing a second check to his young wife, the mute man gestured at the door before turning his back on her.

The blind man took off his dark glasses, gave them to his wife, and said, "I don't have as much money as my friends do, but I offer you my glasses. This way, I'll be with you without you being with me. You can have these glasses, as they don't make any difference in my life, just like you."

The mute man put the blind man's hand on the wheelchair handle of their paralyzed friend. Together, they pushed it into the living room until they were out of sight.

The unexpected visitors had provoked an unexpected reaction, and although they may have picked the fruit they aimed for in their journey of indulgence, they had surely lost face. Now they continued their journey, leaving behind the most precious thing one could have, family and dignity.

10.

FAMILIAL DECISION

In the living room, Liam was switching between channels, bored out of his mind, searching for something worth watching. He wasn't used to staying home—or rather, staying awake for this long. Every dawn, he prepared himself for bed and fell deeply asleep in no time, staying asleep until the sun went down again. Then he would wake up with renewed energy to start his day. At 8:00 p.m. sharp, he got on the road. His neighbors all thought he was a nightshift worker, and Liam certainly was. Well, not a worker exactly, but rather a loyal customer at the Pipe Dream Pub, where he truly felt at home. It was an easy escape from the battlefield of life—although ignoring life's problems became a problem in itself. But with the COVID-19 lockdown, a new issue had arisen; he couldn't go to the place he was fond of or leave the place he felt detached from.

Sitting in front of the TV, Liam began to drowse on the couch. His family of three made an unlooked-for entrance, rousing him, and when they passed by without so much as noticing his presence, his anger woke him up fully. However, he quickly regained his composure and pondered the situation. The only time they knew he was home was when they heard him snoring—so did they think he was just a piece of furniture in the house? Or were they intentionally ignoring him as vengeance for his negligence?

At first glance, Liam almost couldn't tell his wife and daughter apart, they looked so much alike. Had his wife gotten twenty years younger, or had his daughter grown into a beautiful woman? That made him feel as proud as a peacock, but it also made him feel downhearted since she no longer ran to him as a child, like in the good old days he often reminisced about. He called for her, his arms wide open to hug her, but to his disappointment, she only kissed his forehead as she continued her phone call. He couldn't even kiss her back as she seemed to fade into thin air.

The second figure to appear was his son, who Liam noticed had grown a mustache. He greeted his father perfunctorily, without even bothering to stop by, provoking Liam to action. He rushed to his son and tried to attract his attention by mentioning a game cartridge he'd bought him in the past. The son jokingly commented that it had been a few years since he'd last played that game—now considered a collector's item—and that these days, he played virtual reality games. Liam tried to keep up with the conversation but soon realized he had no clue what his son was talking about.

Then it was his wife's turn, who waved to him while she walked by on her way to the kitchen. This delighted Liam; he was certain his wife would be the last person on Earth to abandon him. He even started thinking up romantic words to express his affection. However, as soon as he got to the kitchen and was about to speak up, she quickly shushed him. He felt let down when he noticed her talking to her iPad as she held a molten chocolate cake. Too late, he discovered she had been a well-known YouTuber for some time now.

42

He returned to his couch, the only thing that kept him company. His daughter was busy with her friends, his son with his video games, and his wife with her new project. Their busyness made him realize that he, too, was busy living in his own bubble. Conflicting feelings of frustration, alienation, and regret overtook him, and then a desire to cry and scream burned within.

"I've become a stranger to my own family," he said, bursting into tears.

Suddenly, Liam's features changed from desperate to determined. He looked like a man ready to take on the world. He planted his feet on the floor next to his loyal couch. "I'm not giving up that easily. It's better to start late than to not try at all."

He stood, head held high, declaring as enthusiasm overwhelmed him: "For my family's sake and my honor, I'm going to make a change."

He reached into his pocket, as if to take out a slip of paper in preparation to deliver a historical speech—but pulled out only a silver flask, filled with scotch. He quaffed from it, a grin on his face as he squinted at his wife and children who were tied up with their own lives.

He turned his back to the scene behind him, concluding his grand decision with a long sigh. "Not today, though. Such crucial decisions require deep reflection." He leaned against the staircase railing, staggering up to his bedroom, still sipping from his flask, his old buddy.

11.

BY THE ROADSIDE

Businesses shut down and stock markets crashed. Jobs were lost and empires were shaken, bringing down arrogant heads. Not only did the event take away lives—except those of children for some unapparent reason—but it succeeded in shaking the entire globe, a near impossible task to achieve. But it was a curse in itself, and there was probably nothing to be done about it.

Streets were deserted, shops were closed, and restaurants were desolated. Many declared bankruptcy; even the panhandlers felt sympathetic toward the shop owners. Restrictions on movement were imposed, kickstarting the home delivery business and triggering a sudden motorcycle boom.

"Right away, ma'am!"

Once the restaurant owner hung up from the call, he approached Jack, handing him the address almost tenderly. Jack, the young delivery guy, put the order in the food delivery box before perching on the seat of his fiery red motorcycle, a raucous roar bursting from the wide-open chrome throttle.

Before the exhaust smoke had fully dissipated, the lady called again. "You'd like extra sandwiches, ma'am? The delivery guy has left actually, but it's okay, I'll send them with another."

The restaurant owner called out for Owen, and a gray-haired man pushed back his chair and stood, seemingly bothered by the interruption. He placed the bag in the food delivery box of his ocean-blue motorcycle and flumped onto the seat, his muttering almost overwhelming the roar of the vehicle. As soon as Owen had realized that he was no more than a backup for Jack, it made his blood boil.

"This isn't the first time the owner has preferred him over me, even after my years of experience. I'm far more competent. I know it's because they're related," Owen hissed to himself, eyebrows furrowed. He continued, "If it wasn't for Corona, I wouldn't have lost my job as a stunt driver in top-drawer movies and had to work in a third-rate restaurant in the city. It's time I got back at them! I'll do it for everyone who's oppressed around the world." There was nothing more to be said. He pressed the start button, announcing his head-to-head battle.

Through the side mirror, Jack noticed Owen approaching and smiled contemptuously. His motorcycle was newer, and he was younger. "I only started working in the restaurant to mix with the lower class for a change—now competing with them will even be more exciting!" He flipped down his helmet visor, gunning for the challenge.

At first, Jack stayed ahead of Owen effortlessly thanks to his robust three-hundred-horsepower engine. The streets were empty and almost all the shops were closed, as if their route had turned into a racetrack reserved just for them. However, after a mile or so, Jack was surprised to see that Owen had somehow passed him. As it turned out, Owen had taken a shortcut that only veteran drivers knew of. Jack complained, "Those bastards! When will they understand that there are limits!"

Jack decided to resort to a sophisticated modern device—his GPS. He knew for certain that Owen, an old-fashioned man, didn't use one. This soon gave Jack a narrow lead, but not for long; the GPS guided him through a zigzagging route that slowed him down, and Owen took the lead once more, knowing the surrounding roads inside and out.

Jack stepped on it until he surpassed Owen. He then skidded to a halt, got off his bike, and pushed a garbage bin into the middle of the road to hinder the way of his rival. Then he rushed back on his way to his destination. Even so, Owen managed to make his way through the messy blockade at the last second.

For the second time, they were neck and neck. They soon approached a crossroad, each choosing a different route: Jack relied on his GPS, Owen on his experience.

The two contenders were so focused on winning the race that they failed to realize the routes they took were connected to a zone completely blocked off—Corona-affected. Because of this, an alternative temporary exit merged both their routes together, blindsiding both Jack and Owen. Neither possession of a modern device nor experience alone could have anticipated that out-of-the-blue change.

The conclusion was expected by everyone except the pair: they collided, fell from their vehicles, and were knocked unconscious. Thank goodness the food they carried wasn't ruined. Certainly, it was fortunate for the several homeless people who roamed the area where the accident came to pass. They seized their chance, snatching the food and taking off, considering it a gift sent from above. They left the two rivals lying unconscious by the roadside without a backward glance.

12.

REUNION SOIREE

Her once-captivating red dress grew dirty, her nail polish seemed dull. This wasn't Corona—only what was left of her. The club goers wondered at the change.

She grasped an empty bottle in one hand and a pair of worn high heels in the other. She walked haltingly, fearing that her legs would fail her, for she had drunk herself to numbness. Her eyes could no longer make out what was before her.

"Corona no longer rules," they said. "Corona's days are over," they joked. "Corona is far gone," they concluded.

She wished she could creep into their throats, penetrate their lungs, and strip them bare of their last atoms of oxygen. But she knew they were vaccinated against her. Still, there was a bright side to her misery, as only now was she able to know who her true friends were. Everyone had deserted her except for two: Ebola and SARS.

"I failed," she mumbled to herself, tiredly seating herself in the closest chair.

Ebola snatched the bottle from her hand while SARS helped her put on her shoes.

"I brought about so much death, yet I haven't accomplished the one goal I set for myself." Her voice rose in pitch until it was almost a wail. "I fought to break the record, but I didn't succeed."

Ebola and SARS tried to calm her, but to no avail. Everyone at the club seemed frustrated at this turn of events, including the waiters, who feared that customers would flounce out of the club along with their wallets.

Unsure of what could be done, the club guards stood still. Even though Corona was light as paper, she was also sharp as a paper cut. Indeed, her looks could still take your breath away, her voice embracing your soul tenderly, her scent beckoning you to heaven—but nonetheless, all were wary of going anywhere close to Corona! The guards had learned to live with this.

A glass of water doesn't do much, yet even half a glass can restore energy or help one regain consciousness. This is exactly what happened to Corona when her beautiful face was splashed with chilled water.

Corona leaped up, let out a piercing shriek, and demanded an immediate answer: Who had dared to perpetrate such a blunder? The answer was simple to all and sundry: it was not just another club goer, but the owner himself.

"Well done, there! The number of casualties is not all it's cracked up to be, but you have indeed caused much more chaos than expected. Congrats!" The club owner patted Corona's shoulder. Then he ordered his assistants to fix Corona's makeup, which had been ruined by the sudden splash.

Corona spoke as she began to regain control of herself. "But I haven't killed every infected person!" she whined.

The club owner sat comfortably on a couch opposite a marble table, surrounded by Ebola and SARS, who were busy finishing off their gourmet meal. "You killed something far more essential," he reassured her, "—their confidence in the present, and their hope for a better future. In doing so, they're easily manipulated. It was executed beautifully, whether you were aware of it or not."

The owner continued, addressing everyone at the club, who seemed magnetized by his speech, "Everyone has a role to play, even when you're in the dark about it." He turned to Corona and her two friends as he puffed from his e-cigar, multicolored smoke circling his head like a rainbow. "Even these poor visitors have a role to play—the injured, the paramedic, the spectator, the benefactor, and other countless roles."

"But how does one pick a role for themselves?" Ebola wondered.

Barely holding back a smile, the owner replied, "According to their will. At least, that's what they think."

SARS, trying hard to conceal his admiration, asked the owner, "Why does it feel as though you can see beyond the obvious?"

The praise boosted the owner's pride. "Oh, it isn't much for someone who had the spaceflight that first landed humans on the moon named after him."

Corona choked. "Apollo! You deceived me!"

The club owner—Apollo—stood, his elegant suit disappearing, to reveal a white Grecian robe that dropped to his knees. "As a matter of fact, Corona—or should I call you Daphne—I have succeeded where you have failed: you couldn't escape me!"

Daphne rushed to the club's exit, not wanting to listen to whatever else he had to say.

The guards hesitated to intervene in what seemed to be just another everyday quarrel. Apollo nodded, slowly extending his fist to reveal a few crusty bits of bay leaf. Everyone was sure that the man had lost his mind, and thus somehow felt reassured. Before they knew it, he blew the tiny yellowish crumbs of leaf from his hand, turning the entire place upside down; tables overturned, chairs hurtled about. The club goers were taken aback, their own powerlessness rooting them, mute, to the spot. Their eyes were blinded, their feet frozen in place. Before Daphne could touch the exit door handle, an arrow pierced it, locking it forever.

"It is rare in life to get second chances, particularly at running away," Apollo taunted, his hands clutching his silver bow.

Daphne tried pulling out the arrow, but to no avail. "How can you love someone who hates you?" she retorted.

Apollo stomped toward her. "The deeper the love, the deeper the hate. If the river hadn't dried up, you would never have escaped."

"If my feelings hadn't dried up, the river would have survived," Daphne replied.

The door suddenly burst open, and a young lady strode in. Her beauty appeared to be no less than that of Daphne, yet she seemed shamelessly bolder. Otherwise, she would never have dared to confront or reproach the most legendary archer known to mankind.

"Have I not enticed you enough that you're taking a toll on this poor woman?"

Apollo was clearly shaken by the sight of her. "Cassandra! How did you find me?"

Cassandra stretched out her arms, and two radiantly yellow-eyed snakes slithered from them. Apollo quickly shot two arrows, their blades made of falcon beaks, piercing the hungry snakes.

Cassandra pulled herself together. "Begone! I can tell your end will be dire."

"Had your prophecy been true, your name wouldn't be associated with epics of tragedy," Apollo hurled back.

Daphne was about to remind Apollo of Cassandra's abilities when the latter interrupted, whispering to her, "He's neither the first to doubt me, nor will he be the last, until it's too late. He was caught in the trap he had set himself"

Both Daphne and Cassandra withdrew to the street. Daphne rushed to the fire hydrant but was unable to turn the valve. "Could you lend me a hand, Cassandra? Death is more merciful than staying here with him!"

Cassandra attempted to dispel her apprehension. "Worry not. I see no future for you with him."

Apollo appeared before Daphne with a flash. "Can't you see that the present is telling a different story?" she screamed. "Help me and I'll hold myself accountable for what's to follow."

Cassandra shook her head sadly. A second later, a hefty snake crawled from beneath her purple dress, wrapping itself around the fire hydrant, the pressure gathering until it shattered, and water burst out like a roaring waterfall. Once Daphne sank her hand into the flowing water, her palm became instantly covered in bay leaves. Her fingers transformed into branches, and small, blackberry-like fruits sprouted from her nails.

"The greatest mistake you could ever make is repeating one," Cassandra forewarned.

Without warning, the sky began raining arrows of all colors and sizes, as though Apollo had lost his mind, until the water from the fire hydrant was blocked off entirely.

"Your transformation into a tree will eternalize my sorrow. Therefore, I must dismiss you from my mind to bring me rest, but this can happen only with your death," Apollo threatened.

The two companions were struck with arrows, willingly sacrificing themselves in solidarity. Apollo apparently could not have cared less, as he continued to shoot a barrage of arrows toward them.

Then, a gentle breeze blew through the open space as a ringing of bells was heard. A woman who bore a strong resemblance to Apollo, riding a chariot pulled by four golden-horned deer, flew across the heavens.

"I warn you, Artemis!" Apollo spoke. "You altered the course of events by shooting healing arrows down Earth's way which helped discover vaccines. Do not intervene again. This is not your battle."

Her chariot approached the two women, who hopped in like a shot. "You and I are bound by blood, while these ladies and I are bound by honor. We vowed eternal chastity, which you sought to besmirch."

Apollo drew his bow to discharge two arrows dripping with blood. "Then they must die before they bring about the end of our eternal bond."

Artemis waved her scarf. The clouds clustered together until the sky grew dark, blocking the moonlight. Soon it became pitch black, rendering Apollo blind as a bat. He released hundreds of flaming arrows until the clouds ripped apart and his vision cleared.

Too late, he spotted his twin sister, accompanied by Cassandra and Daphne within the chariot, winging its way to the vicinity of the moon. He kept his bow arm steady, gazing at his target, biding his time to shoot—but soon they were out of his sight, out of his reach, and out of his life.

EPILOGUE

In his quest to lay hold of the chariot that whizzed over the moon, Apollo shot a grappling hook, then used the rope to get atop the moon.

There he saw something that sent a chill down his spine: three bodiless faces debating zealously back and forth.

Apollo swallowed his suddenly dry throat. "Who are you?"

The eldest of them, unbonneted and with short-cropped hair as white as snow, matching his abundant beard, retorted, "We are the residents, whereas you are a guest, which gives us the prerogative to ask your identity first. In any case, I am the mentee of Socrates and the mentor of Aristotle."

"Plato?" Apollo inquired in admiration.

Plato nodded. "And these are my two tutees—although they were several hundred years late for my classes." He pointed to his left, where an old man who looked to be in his seventies stood. He wore a jet-black turban that complemented his ghost-white French forked beard, and his eyes glowed with passion. "Averroes," he introduced himself.

Plato then gestured to an astute man, only slightly younger, on his right to draw nearer. He wore a sudra wrapped in a turban that caressed his grayish goatee. "Maimonides," Plato presented.

Apollo introduced himself. "I'm Apollo, and I came here looking for three women who I'm certain passed by you. Have you seen them?"

"Do you know them?" Averroes asked, as if to trip him up.

Bluntly, Apollo answered, "If I hadn't known them, I wouldn't have asked about them."

In a continued effort to make him slip, Maimonides commented, "Had you known them, you would have realized why they left."

Apollo dropped to his knees with a sense of defeat. "Had I really known them, they wouldn't give me such agitation. They didn't understand my philosophy, I love to love, but I love being loved more. Only for the sake of love do I love, never for whom I love."

"What sane person could be fond of his victimizer?" Plato remarked. "Unless you were the one who sowed the seeds of your own distress."

Apollo was silent.

"I assume your silence can be read as assent," Plato remarked.

"Why have you treated them in such a manner?" Averroes said, anger now in his voice.

Maimonides seemed more inquisitive. "And how?"

Red-faced, Apollo replied, "Why? I loved the first one, and the second worked to erase any trace of my old love." His tone gradually sharpened. "How? I've been kind, but kindness didn't bring them back, so I threatened instead; thus, they sought my sister's powers to save their skins. Little did they know that my deed stemmed from love."

"You deemed them ignorant to justify your vengeance. Ignorance leads to fear, fear leads to hate, and hate leads to violence. This is the equation," Averroes said disapprovingly.

Maimonides was united in his opinion. "An ignorant man believes that the whole universe only exists for him, as if nothing else required any consideration."

"Easy, you two!" Plato interrupted. "You don't reward him who owns up to his fault by condemning him."

Apollo's chin lowered to his chest. "I plead guilty, even if my actions were done in good faith."

Plato corrected him. "Or were they done in the name of pleasure? A most mighty lure to evil."

Apollo's tone was obstinate. "Pleasure and guilt are but different sides of the same picture. I sought their death to cleanse that guilt and cut them from my life."

"How do you take action when you're blindsided?" Maimonides scolded him disdainfully. "It is better and more satisfactory to acquit a thousand guilty persons than to put a single innocent one to death."

"I am the son of Zeus the great! It's within my rights to carry out his wishes," Apollo bragged.

Maimonides cut him short. "What makes you believe that is what he wishes for? Have you asked him? We suffer from evils which we, by our own free will, inflict on ourselves and ascribe them to God, who is far from being connected with them!"

Scratching his forehead, Apollo asked, "And how can I know if my actions please God?"

"The true work of God is all good, since it is existence itself," Maimonides said.

Apollo fell silent a second time.

Reading Apollo's face, Averroes commented, "It appears that this time, his silence speaks a different answer."

"Silence is a fence around wisdom," Maimonides seconded.

Apollo breathed a sigh of relief. "I feel as though I've been reborn. What advice do you give me before I'm gone?"

Plato wore a grin from ear to ear. "A young man who has just arrived from Earth will bestow that advice upon you."

A Chinese man, accompanied by two brightly pearl-colored angels whose wings encompassed him in a motherly fashion, came into view.

"He was the subject of our debate before your arrival took us by surprise," Averroes added.

"Who is he?" Apollo's curiosity was heightened.

"Li Wenliang," answered Averroes.

"And what has he done to be elevated to such a prominent level? Is he a philosopher?"

"In action, he is indeed," Plato replied.

Li Wenliang addressed Apollo. "I sacrificed myself for the greater good of humanity."

"What led you to do that?"

"I followed the path of the aphorism of my teacher, Confucius: What you do not wish for yourself, do not do unto others."

But their wisdom did not quench Apollo's thirst. He therefore decided to stick around for more. He proceeded to cut the rope connecting him to Earth, but upon his return, he was astonished to see the souls of the philosophers and Li Wenliang soar to the heavens above, emerging as stars.

Apollo sat, put away his bow, and brought out his lyre. He began to play, and he still plays it now—the only language that all humans understand.

ABOUT THE AUTHOR

The author is a soul that had no hand in determining its birth-date, dwelling, or gender, and most certainly not the day it will bite the dust—the matter which draws all souls closer.

Yet those very same souls are born with free will... they either fall into good or evil, turn out fruitful or unhelpful, and evolve as humans or half humans—the matter which sets all souls apart.